Friday Adventures

Friday Adventures

PV Jackson

ISBN 978-1-9399304-7-7

LCCN 2017955519

Cover Illustration by KR Jackson

Printed in the United States

Published by

Brandylane Publishers, Inc.
WWW.BRANDYLANEPUBLISHERS.COM

To the three sweet girls who give my life meaning

CONTENTS

Chapter One

Kate

Kate adjusted herself in the harness. She drifted dreamily in the canopy. She loved being in the trees. The air was warm but not unpleasant. A slight breeze shifted her position as the ropes made groaning and pinging sounds under her weight.

"Where have you gone to?" she asked. A slight movement caught her quick eyes. "There you are, Mr. Longshot! I knew you couldn't have gone far."

Kate reached over and picked up the beetle. To most observers, it would be just a beetle. If asked, Kate would have said that this was one of the most beautiful creatures in the world. It had an unusually long cephalothorax that seemed to help it balance as it traveled the leaves of the upper canopy. Kate's team was still waiting on a final decision from the International Commission of Zoological Nomenclature about whether this beetle could be considered a new species. If so, this could be a big deal. Kate might even be named as a co-author of the paper her team was finalizing. But regardless of the official binomial nomenclature, the beetle would always be "Mr. Longshot" to Kate.

A faint buzzing sensation came from one of Kate's pockets, and Kate was annoyed. She didn't like to be disturbed when she was in the canopy. Since she had arrived in Costa Rica, her time in the treetops had become precious. Her experiences in the harness were the closest thing to flying that she could imagine. Whenever she entered the canopy, she felt a thrill of excitement and adventure unlike anything she had ever experienced on land. Only surfing came close to the exhilaration she felt as she ascended the trees. Adding to the gravity of her physical exertions was the fact that she was doing important work—important scientific work. Up here, her world was right.

The persistent buzzing didn't stop. "For crying out loud!" She clenched her teeth as she tried to reposition so she could reach her cell phone. After a minute, she put the old phone to her ear, still annoyed.

"Kate, you have a video call down here." Mara's voice was scratchy over the ancient cell phone. The phone really was only good for local walkie-talkie communication, and not useful as a satellite phone in the field. "I think it's your sister."

"What in the world?" Kate whispered to herself as she began her descent. Her sister, Grace, rarely called her, especially when Kate was on a research assignment. A vague sense of unease cramped her stomach. Fleeting thoughts of tragedy raced through her mind, but she quickly tamped them down. They had suffered enough recently—or so she hoped.

Kate reached the ground and removed the harness. She anxiously approached the base camp mess tent, where external communications were received. The satellite link provided excellent video communications, despite their remote location. Kate tapped the refresh button and her sister's face filled the screen. Grace grinned sheepishly. Despite her annoyance at having been called away from her work, Kate felt a warm surge of affection for her sister. Grace seemed relaxed, so Kate relaxed a bit herself. No tragedy this time, it would seem.

"What in the world?" Kate said. "Is everything okay?"

Grace nodded. "Don't worry. Everything is fine. I hate to bother you at work, but when are you coming home?" She had a sly, mischievous look on her face.

Kate was again annoyed. She had made her travel plans clear to Grace and Mom before leaving the US. She would be in Costa Rica for another week of fieldwork before returning to the US to finish her part of the data analysis. Kate's master's thesis would derive from the work she was finishing now. Time was of the essence. Her funding would be exhausted soon, and she would be forced to return to the university whether she was finished or not. Her team hoped to publish a significant paper and seek further funding based on this trip. Academics, now more than ever, existed on the "publish or perish" premise—very Darwinian.

"I plan to be back in Richmond in three weeks or so. Why? What's up? How's Mom?"

Grace hesitated a beat. She had probably seen Kate tense on the video. "Mom is fine, as far as I know. She's still in Haiti. I spoke with her last week." Their mother worked as a nurse and was on a medical mission in Haiti with her employer and his family.

Kate was getting a bit impatient. It was nice talking with her sister, whom she had not seen in weeks, but she had work to do.

"And?" Kate prompted.

"She's fine. That's not why I called." Grace started to grin, and Kate started to get impatient. She knew her sister loved to drag things out. Ever since they were kids, Kate always seemed to have to wait for her sister.

"You're not married, are you? What is it already?"

"No, I'm not married," Grace said. She took a deep breath. "I received something in the mail today."

Kate felt her mouth go dry. "What is it?"

"I haven't opened it yet. The instructions say that

we have to open it together."

Kate was silent for a moment. Puzzled, she glanced out of the mess tent and into the canopy that she loved. She had an odd feeling. What was her sister talking about? What could this thing be? What could it mean? She felt a sudden, inexplicable tangle of emotions.

"What do you think it is?" she asked Grace.

"When can you come home?" Grace asked gently.

"I can't possibly get home for another week. Just tell me what you think it is."

Grace nodded her head and said, "I think it's from Dad."

Chapter Two

Grace

Grace was both happy and sad that the semester was over. She always felt mixed emotions when school ended for a term. She liked school. She was good at academic work. She thoroughly enjoyed her vacations, but she was never really upset when school started again.

She considered her options for the summer. She had a chance to intern for the advertising agency again. She had enjoyed the creativity and the electric atmosphere she had felt in her (sadly, unpaid) position there. Now that she was in college, she also considered volunteering to gain experience. But she wanted gainful employment now.

She could always go back to work at the ice cream shop. Within walking distance of her home, the shop had been her place of employment for several years during high school, and she liked the happy vibe of the place. Everyone enjoyed ice cream. Grace had liked learning the business side of the food industry. She was a good cook. Her mother constantly watched cooking shows and was an excellent cook herself. She liked trying new things, and Grace had started baking cupcakes with her at an early age.

It was in the kitchen that she had sorted the mail after picking it up from the box at the top of the driveway. An envelope had caught her attention. It was a business envelope, hand-addressed to her and her sister. The writing was familiar, and Grace felt a thrill when she looked at the return address. In the upper left hand corner was written a single word:

Beyond.

Chapter Three

Translations

Kate leaned against a window in the San Jose airport and took another sip of her bottled water. Travel was fatiguing, and she was relieved that she had not gotten sick while in Costa Rica. She had feared illness, especially GI illness, and any embarrassment that might have followed. Kate was a very private person.

Looking at her reflection in the window, she could tell that she had gotten some sun. She appeared tan and fit, having gained some wiry muscle definition in her arms from climbing. Although she was short compared to some, at five-foot-two, she liked her proportions. Her blond hair had grown even more silvery in the Costa Rican sun. She let her hair fall around her shoulders, instead of putting it up in her usual ponytail, now that she no longer needed to worry about snagging it on trees in the canopy.

As she waited for her flight, Kate reflected on her

time in Costa Rica. She had jumped at the opportunity to join her graduate school team on their research trip. She was fortunate enough to be able to afford those expenses not covered by the grant funding, and had even been able to arrange an extra two weeks of immersive Spanish language training, which her mother had encouraged as a way to really internalize the language. She had taken Latin in school, so she found the structure and rhythms of Spanish familiar. To her surprise, she had even started to dream in Spanish, as her mother had predicted.In the end, Kate had had no trouble communicating with people she encountered in her travels, and found that they appreciated her efforts to speak Spanish. She and one of her fellow graduate students, Mara, had lived for two weeks with an elderly couple named Morales in a village outside of San Jose, in a modest house with members of several generations of the family. The rooms of the house were separated with fabric curtains.

Upon their arrival, Kate and Mara had been welcomed by the villagers with a dance held in a local barn. They were both delighted and humbled by the sincere affection and hospitality shown to them by these good people, especially la familia Morales. Though poor by American standards, they gave generously of what they had, and made the girls feel like family.

Part of the girls' language and cultural education had involved local travel. One of the first emotions that had struck Kate was terror, as they traveled the treacherous roads. Frequent rains had left the roads in a state of seemingly perpetual disrepair, and she had been advised to drive only during the day, for fear of not seeing the sometimes huge holes that could develop. Potholes weren't the only worry: the Morales children took great delight in telling Kate how to avoid the fer-de-lance snakes that could pose a danger to her in her work.

Kate and Mara had toured local coffee plantations and learned of local agriculture. At one point, they came to a small river that smelled so strongly of human waste that they smelled it before they saw it. It ran down from another village higher up in the hills. There was no bridge across the water, so to cross the river, Kate paid a man (who surely had the strongest immune system in the cosmos) the equivalent of fifty cents to wade into the river and pull her and Mara across in a small boat.

Despite this one adventure in hygiene, Kate was impressed with the beauty of Costa Rica and its focus on natural resources, including its large and well-respected system of national parks. The environmentally conscious agriculture seemed to blend seamlessly into the landscape. Even goat farmers used living teakwood fences to corral their herds. Kate felt a natural kinship with those who loved and respected nature, and had also been impressed by the fidelity with which Senora Morales recited the Angelus at 6:00 a.m. and 6:00 p.m. daily. Remembering the love and belonging she had witnessed in these virtual strangers gave her more than a twinge of regret, and made her feel somewhat guilty that she had not called her mom recently. She would have to do so when she arrived in Richmond.

Chapter Four

Transitions

Grace didn't know what to do with herself. For the first time in her life, she felt an odd sense of drifting, completely alone. She knew that it was only temporary. Kate and Mom would both return home soon, and she would return to school next semester. Her future was secure. That was what she told herself, but for the immediate present, she was isolated, untethered. Although faintly melancholy, it was not a completely unpleasant feeling. She imagined herself in a small safe house on the edge of a vast unknown, peeking out at what could be over the next hill, just out of sight. Beyond.

Grace walked aimlessly through the house. She wandered into her bedroom, went to her desk, and picked up a framed picture of herself and her best friend Taylor. Grace saw her fading freckles and coppery hair framing her smiling face. She and her friend looked happy.

Grace liked her possessions and always had trouble parting with anything. Her mom loved order and tidiness, and Grace had inherited the same trait, which constantly clashed with her tendency to be a pack rat. She understood this about herself. Two conflicting natures seemed to compete for her attention: order and something else. Chaos, she supposed. Yet, in the messy, cluttered, distinctly untidy places, she felt her creativity move.

Grace wondered if she should make some food for Kate's visit. Kate would probably appreciate home cooking after traveling. She considered the possibilities, planning the preparations in her mind.

She hesitated before leaving her room though. For this one bittersweet moment, she actually wanted to linger a bit, all alone.

Chapter Five

Beyond

Kate and Grace looked at the box. Neither of them wanted to open it just yet. It wasn't fear or dread. It was anticipation—like the kind that came on Christmas morning, the moment before they opened their presents. The thrill of that anticipation was often better than the present itself. They grinned at each other.

"What do you think it is?" Kate asked Grace.

"It's heavy," Grace replied as she lifted the package. Within the cardboard box, something shifted with a solid thump. The package had arrived as promised, two weeks after the letter from "Beyond."

Together, the girls read the letter again. It was a single page, handwritten but unsigned—

Kate and Grace,
In two weeks, a package will
arrive at this same address.
Please open the package together
and follow the instructions.

Grace picked up a pair of scissors. "Ready?"
Kate nodded.

Grace opened the box deftly. She took out an object covered in bubble wrap, gently removed the protective wrapping, and exposed something familiar. She felt a gasp escape her lips, and heard her sister do the same.

It was an old laptop computer, white and smooth—the same computer that had rested for years on their father's desk. The two sisters had both learned basic computer skills on this very computer. They had spent hours making videos of themselves performing skits and commercials with fanciful names like "Scented Socks" and "The Skeleton Show". It was during this time that Grace had first become interested in making movies, which had eventually led to her interest in advertising and art.

Grace removed the power cable and plugged it into the wall outlet. She guided the adapter to the computer and felt a magnetic click as the power cable connected. She opened the top and pressed the power button, and the computer came to life.

After the machine booted up, a dialogue box asked for the password. Grace looked at writing on the masking tape at the bottom of the keyboard and typed it in. The electronic desktop appeared. There was only one icon on the desktop, and she clicked it.

A moment passed. Then, a video started.

"Hello, girls. I'm speaking to you from beyond the grave! I bet you never thought you'd hear from me again!" Their father's face smiled mischievously from the computer screen. Kate and Grace both felt their throats tighten. Tears came to their eyes as they looked again at their father. He paused a moment as he looked into the camera that captured his image. Unspoken, but evident nonetheless, was a depth of feeling and emotion that played upon his tired face.

"Try not to be too sad that I'm gone. Everyone has to die. But if you have to die, you might as well have some fun with it."

"I hope you're happy and well, my sweet girls. There is so much I wish I could say, but I have brought you together today for a purpose." He seemed to brighten a bit as the grin returned to his face. "Foremost, I want to thank you both. I enjoyed hanging out with you guys. Indeed, here at the end of my life, some of my fondest memories are from the times we spent together on our Friday Adventures. Remember those? Your mom was at work and I looked after you. Just as my father had taken me all over the city of Richmond, I took you to some of my favorite places. We saw things, did things, tried new foods. We had fun." His voice cracked a little as he spoke. "I know your lives must be busy now but, for old times' sake, I would like for us to go on one last set of Friday Adventures."

He took a deep breath and paused. He looked to be in pain for a moment, and then it seemed to pass. "When you were little, your mom used to make scavenger hunts for prizes and treats on Easter morning. She worked late into the night putting up the decorations and hiding the clues that would lead you to your treats. I had great fun watching you follow the clues to your Easter baskets. I have taken this as my model for our last Friday Adventure." He paused again and looked earnestly at the camera.

"Here's what let's do..."

Chapter Six

Six Degrees of Separation

The video continued. "In the 1990s, there was an actor named Kevin Bacon. He was a prolific actor—he starred in the original *Footloose*, by the way—and was jokingly referred to as 'the center of the acting universe.' It was said that any other actor could be linked to him in six steps or less. For example, let's start with one of your favorite cartoon characters:

SpongeBob SquarePants, who was in *The SpongeBob SquarePants Movie* with King Neptune's daughter Princess Mindy, whose voice was provided by actress...

Scarlett Johansson, who was in the movie *Lost in Translation* with actor...

Bill Murray, who was on the TV show *Saturday Night Live* with actor...

John Belushi, who was in the 1978 movie *Animal House* with actor...

Kevin Bacon

"See how this works?

"I would like to propose a similar premise. I think that your mother has been the center of our little universe. I will use our Friday Adventures as proof of this. I will give you a starting point. Then you must find connections that lead from that starting point to your mother. One rule is that each series of connections must include a Richmond landmark that we have visited. The connection to the Richmond landmark will never simply be that your mother visited there. I may send you clues to help you along the way. Remember, the path will lead from the starting point, through a Richmond landmark, and end with your mother. The journey may take more or less than six steps, but that is not the important point. The important point is that you girls work on this together. Spend time together. Visit the places we visited in the past. You may learn some things along the way. I suggest that you touch base at least once a week to discuss your progress — might I suggest Friday? And in the end, there will be treasure. Real treasure."

He paused again, looking as if he didn't want this little joke to end. "There will be three of these puzzles. I'll start off with an easy one first. Good luck and have fun! Are you ready for your first clue? The first starting point is…Swannanoa."

Chapter Seven

Swannanoa

They looked at each other.

"I have no idea what that is," said Kate.

"Neither do I. Let's look it up." Grace took out her handheld computer and brought up the search engine. "How do you spell it? Swan-a-know-a?" Grace typed a few letters into her device and exclaimed, "Ah, here we go! Swannanoa. Let's see…there's a Swannanoa in North Canterbury, New Zealand. Dad would have liked anything with Canterbury in it." Their father had been a bit of an Anglophile; even now, Kate could recall the British flag he kept in his office. "'Keep Calm and Carry On,'" Grace said, reciting one of their dad's favorite phrases from World War II-era Britain. "There's also a 'Lake Swannanoa' in New Jersey. There's a Swannanoa River in North Carolina. Wait! There's an estate called Swannanoa in Virginia. This must be it." Grace scanned a few lines of text and said, "Swannanoa was the summer home of Sallie and James Dooley. 'Completed in 1913, the Italianate thirty-nine-room,

22,000-square-foot mansion presided over a 761-acre estate on Afton Mountain.'" Grace concentrated for a moment. "'Dooley.' That name sounds familiar."

Kate could see Grace's mind turning. She knew that Grace possessed a prodigious, almost photographic memory. Grace typed a few more queries into her computer. "Yes, I thought so. The Dooley mansion." She looked up at her sister. "Our first Richmond landmark must be Maymont."

Kate and Grace discussed the logistics of what they wanted to do. Kate had to finish some important work for her research team. She didn't want to delay her portion of the write-up, lest they miss their publication deadline. It always seemed that she was under some type of deadline. She often went days without seeing or talking to anyone outside of her work group, and she sometimes got so focused on her work that she forgot to eat and worked throughout the night without realizing she had missed a whole night of sleep—not to mention her uncanny ability to hold her urine. She could pass a whole day and not go to the bathroom. She referred to this as her superpower. Some superheroes had super-strength or invisibility; Kate's power was owning the strongest bladder in the western hemisphere.

The girls decided that Grace would continue to research the Dooleys, looking for connections to their mother. The girls would meet the following Friday to tour Maymont. They had no real idea of what they were supposed to do or look for. The video offered no further instructions.

Grace decided to read up on Maymont and the Dooleys in preparation for the visit. Her job at the ice cream shop could wait a while. This would be more fun.

Kate gave Grace some advice to help her in her research. "This will be more like social science qualitative research. I suggest that you document your sources, using APA guidelines for your references." Kate could never resist her instinct to provide references for any research she performed. "Better safe than sorry" was her philosophy, and she had done enough research that her inner radar for possible publication material was pinging.

The girls agreed to keep in touch as their trip to Maymont approached. Kate departed her childhood home with a wave, leaving Grace in the kitchen.

This whole situation was weird, Grace thought. Weird, odd, and totally cool! What in the world of muscular strength was she supposed to do with this? With her mom out of the country for another week or so and no schoolwork to occupy her, she decided to treat this like a school project. She would research the topics her dad had suggested, document and reference her work in American Psychological Association style as Kate had suggested, and see if she could find some treasure. Grace was confident that if there was a puzzle or mystery to be solved, she could do it. Just as some people were tall, Grace was smart, and she accepted that fact without vanity. She had inherited her dad's love of books. Trips to the bookstore were constant rewards for good grades and special celebrations. While Mom had been the inspiration for hard work and Grace's "get-the-job-done" work ethic, her dad had inspired her love of creativity, reading, and writing.

She missed him. She would sometimes go into his office and sit among his books and papers, hoping to notice an object or catch a whiff of some scent that would remind her of him. She had seen him do the same thing with an old spice rack in their kitchen. Tucked in that spice rack were handwritten recipes that his mother had saved throughout her life. Grace had noticed that on some occasions—holidays especially—her father would open the drawer of the spice rack not to read the recipes, but just to smell the scent coming from the drawer. "It smells like her," he would say with a look of thoughtfulness.

Grace went upstairs to her father's office. The door was shut. Strangely, a large metal knocker was mounted on the door. Grace had never thought to ask why an interior room would have a knocker. If she had asked, she would have learned that the knocker had been a gift from her father's sister and, not knowing what else to do with it, he had mounted it on his office door.

Ignoring the knocker, Grace opened the door and went in. The room had been built over the garage, and was oddly shaped, long and narrow, with walls that began to slant about four feet or so up from the floor. A set of exquisite handmade cherry bookcases, handmade by her grandfather, ran the full length of one wall. The bookcases were filled to overflowing with books of all shapes and sizes, along with various other curiosities: an old-fashioned windup clock, a human skull (a reproduction?), statues and figurines, candles, and a Robin Hood-style hat hanging on a statue of a wolf. Now that she was older, Grace realized that her dad had had unusual tastes.

She looked at the books. Mysteries, biographies, literature, several Bibles and religious books, textbooks, cookbooks, and quite a few series filled the shelves. The books were not well organized, but they were grouped together by general theme. She found a cache of history books on the bookshelf farthest from the door, closest to a large desk that took up a good portion of the room. Like the bookcases, the desk was made of cherry wood, though unlike the bookcases, it was of a more modern construction, with drawers to accommodate computer accessories. However, the style was French country. The desk had been a gift from Mom. For years, the white computer had rested and worked there. Now, that computer was the catalyst for a treasure hunt.

"Kinkerly Shoetopple," Grace said aloud without thinking. She smiled at herself as she remembered this character from a skit she used to perform. Pleasant memories of her childhood crowded out more recent, less pleasant memories of her dad's illness, decline, and death. She had a sudden memory of herself sitting in her dad's leather desk chair, working on another of her commercials (this one for *Exploding! Beds!*) using the computer's video recorder.

Grace felt an overwhelming desire to bring the computer back to its original resting place and look at her old videos. She missed spending time with Kate, with whom she had filmed many of her commercials, including *Exploding! Beds!* and, of course, (who could forget) *Scented Socks*.

She was about to go downstairs to retrieve the computer when she noticed, among the history books, a collection of books about Richmond, including several books about its history and landmarks. This would be where she would begin her search. Immediately, she understood exactly what her father had done. He had researched to create the puzzles, so she would recreate his search, using his sources, to solve the riddles. After she watched *Exploding! Beds!* that is.

Chapter Eight

Maymont

They parked at the Hampton Street entrance, one of three entrances to the lush, once-private estate of Maymont. Stone-block pillars supported a large iron gate that was now open. An asphalt walkway led to the estate. Almost immediately to the left was a stone patio lined with wood and iron benches. Information kiosks were set up in the center of the patio, which was surrounded by large shrubs, creating the illusion of an outdoor room.

The girls knew that Maymont was richly landscaped. The estate was large at just over one hundred acres, and included the grazing land of a former dairy farm. They had visited many times before, but this time was different. They saw things from a different perspective. Now, they almost felt as if they were studying the place, noticing things that they hadn't noticed before.

They sat on one of the benches to review their plan of action.

"What do we know so far?" Kate asked Grace.

"The Dooleys purchased the land in 1886," Grace replied. She thumbed through a brown notebook with a smooth cardboard cover, which held the notes she had jotted down as she looked through her dad's books and ran computer searches.

She glanced at Kate. Looking at her notes, Grace said, "Well, following Dad's formula, we began with:

Swannanoa, which was built by...

James and Sallie May Dooley, who also built the Richmond landmark...

Maymont.

"Now here we are," finished Kate. She had many fond memories of Maymont, and some not so fond. She remembered busting her lip when she had wiped out on one of the many hills dotting the estate. Sometimes, the entire property seemed to be uphill in every direction. Walking Maymont definitely tested one's level of fitness.

Kate's wipeout was now forever memorialized by the first charm on her charm bracelet. Until she and Grace had turned twelve, their parents had presented each of their girls a gold charm on her birthday, depicting some important interest or event from her life the year before. The bracelet, symbolizing her childhood, was given to each girl on her thirteenth birthday. The very first charm Kate had received was a charm of the Dooley mansion at Maymont.

Kate asked, "Other than the fact that Mom visited here, which we can't use, what connections does she have to the Dooleys or Maymont?"

Grace thought for a moment and replied, "There are several possibilities at this point. The Dooleys were married in Staunton." Grace ran her finger over her notes, where she had recorded, in APA style: O'Leary, 2003 in her notes. "Mom has an uncle in Staunton, but that seems a stretch. Mr. and Mrs. Dooley were married in a private home in Staunton by a Catholic priest. He was Catholic, and she was Episcopalian. Evidently, weddings of Protestants and Catholics were relatively rare in those days. Mom and Dad were similar, in that Mom is Catholic, while Dad was Lutheran. I doubt that's the connection, but it is a similarity. The Dooleys were also active in the parish of St. Peter Catholic Church, which was where Mom and Dad were married. Grace smiled enthusiastically.

"Actually, the Dooleys were a very interesting couple. Everyone focuses on their wealth, and they were wealthy, but they were accomplished as well. Mr. Dooley graduated first in his class at Georgetown. He wasn't really a major, but he was given that honorific title later in life. He actually served as a private in the Confederate army, and was wounded in the Battle of Williamsburg during the Civil War. He was a prisoner of war for a time; then he worked as a lawyer and notary public. After the war, he notarized statements from former Confederates as they swore allegiance to the US Constitution. He also served in the Virginia General Assembly for six years. He made most of his money in the railroad business during Reconstruction."

Grace continued. "Mrs. Dooley was a published author. She published a book called *Dem Good Ole Times* about life in the Gilded Age South. She personally oversaw the creation of the gardens at Maymont, including the arboretum, which I know you like." Grace glanced at Kate, who nodded. Kate had always loved the outdoors, especially trees. "They had no children, and left much of their fortune to charities. They donated Maymont to the City of Richmond to be used as a park, which is why it remains virtually intact today. They gave large bequests to St. Joseph's Villa, and significant gifts to what is now VCU and Children's Hospital of Richmond. Mrs. Dooley also helped found the city's public library." Grace paused. "One of these days, I would love to look through the archives of the Virginia Historical Society to see some of the Dooley papers."

Families and couples streamed into Maymont past the girls as they talked. Finally, Kate stood up.

Grace said, "Are we ready to go, Commander?"

Kate grinned, remembering how her dad had called her "Commander" whenever she took the lead during their adventures. Together, she and Grace stepped deeper into Maymont.

As they walked down the asphalt path, they passed a private house on the left. Kate wondered if the estate's caretakers lived there. Past the private residence was a stone building with a formal herb garden, and they followed the brick path into the garden, which was framed with boxwoods. Upon closer inspection, Kate noted that the garden resembled an old-fashioned physic garden. Large rosemary bushes, apothecary roses, sage, society garlic, mint, bronze fennel, chives, Italian parsley, oregano, lemon balm, and thyme grew in geometric patterns. Black-and-yellow bumblebees worked the different varieties of lavender, one of their mother's favorite herbs. Horehound, feverfew, bee balm, and alpine strawberries had been arranged with methodical care in the patterned garden, which also boasted a sundial in its center and large topiaries, placed thoughtfully at intervals. Iron benches, some saying "In memory of . . ." ringed the periphery.

The girls went farther down the asphalt walkway, past other structures, to a large white alabaster fountain. Surrounded by a columned balustrade, the fountain shot a powerful stream of water twenty feet into the air. Both girls remembered lingering by the pool as their father had used the comfort station with the stone walkway leading to the men's bathroom. He seemed to go to the bathroom a lot. In retrospect, they now realized that probably had significance.

Grace looked out onto the broad lawn that separated the fountain from the nature center, which was barely visible on the other side of the estate. She had noticed advertisements for "Venomous Snakes of Virginia," which must be the newest attraction at the nature center. Maymont had a large array of natural and manmade attractions, including an aviary; exhibits showcasing foxes, bears, bobcats, bison, deer, raptors; and now, evidently, poisonous snakes. The estate featured a children's farm, a butterfly trail, and a vegetable patch near the Spottswood Road entrance. It also boasted a Japanese garden, an Italian garden, a grotto, and a peaceful waterfall. Grace remembered searching through the estate's bamboo forest for the stone lions supposedly hidden within.

And, of course, there was also the Dooley mansion.

The girls walked past the mansion's carriage house, with its collection of broughams, sleighs, and buggies, as well as a horse-drawn hearse with a wicker casket inside. As they made their way down the walkway, they saw the Dooley mansion. Also called Maymont House, the impressive home with its walls of rough stone stood like a castle on a hilltop, overlooking the estate. Although the sisters had been to Maymont many times, they had never taken the Maymont House tour, so they decided to do so, and went to the small basement gift shop, which sold only ornaments and a few books, to register.

After registering for the tour, the girls went to some of the displays housed in the basement. A video told the story of the house and estate, although the girls already knew much of the information from Grace's research. However, the rest of the exhibits in the basement raised other issues that they hadn't considered. Running an estate such as Maymont, or any large facility for that matter, took much effort. The Dooleys had lived through a period of tremendous social and technological change. Major Dooley started his life in the time of slavery and landed gentry, came of age during the Civil War, and made his fortune during Reconstruction. The household of his youth had been supported by a slave economy. However, by the time he had become a wealthy adult, his household had been sustained not by slaves, but by employed laborers.

It took the work of many employees to run a large house such as Maymont. Technological innovations utilized at Maymont included electricity, as well as gas lighting, elevators, and state-of-the-art cooking and heating equipment. The exhibit in the basement of Maymont House focused on the people who made Maymont function, but who were themselves virtually invisible. Kate noticed that most of the employees were female, and most were African-American. She wondered what the working conditions had been like in a place such as Maymont during the Gilded Age.

A bell sounded, signaling the start of their tour, and the girls went to meet the docent, who would act as their tour guide, in the gift shop. The docent was a distinguished-looking middle-aged woman impeccably dressed in business attire, and once everyone had gathered, she led the small tour group along a coral-colored brick path to the large wooden door leading into Maymont House.

Their first steps into the Dooley mansion were breathtaking. From the small foyer, the group could see into numerous rooms. Viewing the rooms of Maymont House was like looking through a kaleidoscope. Each room was lavish and utterly different.

To the left of the foyer was a sitting room decorated in light Brazilian wood. To the right was a study decked out in mahogany, including the window blinds. Within sat a writing table; bookshelves; several Oriental vases; and an eye-catching, intricately carved Italian chair shaped more like a bathtub than a traditional chair. Relief carvings of Poe and

Longfellow decorated a fireplace on one of the walls.

Most of the rooms were roped off. Gray industrial carpet covered the Persian rugs and wood floors, protecting the rich furnishings and structure from the crowds visiting the house. The docent explained that oils from the visitors' skin could damage the art and furniture, as she kept a wary eye on the two-year-old in the group, who wanted to touch everything (and who was eventually taken out of the tour by her mother).

The girls followed the tour guide through the house. Marble statues, often of women and children or childlike cherubs, featured prominently in many rooms. Though childless, the Dooleys seemed to have wanted children. The group toured through the dining room, which was dominated by a huge rosewood-carved china cabinet modeled on one that had stood in the White House at the time. The nook in which it stood had been specifically designed to hold the piece, which had been obtained before the house was constructed. The china cabinet held exquisite handmade and hand-painted china, including oyster plates, each piece a signed work of art.

The tour eventually came to the main entrance hallway, which was where distinguished guests would have entered the house. This foyer was made to impress. A large carved lion guarded the staircase, and any visitor would have immediately been drawn to the large Tiffany stained-glass window that was visible from all three floors of the house. The religious theme of the stained-glass window added to the cathedral-like feel of this part of the mansion.

The tour went up the stairs to the Dooley family's living and sleeping quarters. James and Sallie May Dooley had separate bedrooms. Sallie May's bedroom featured a whimsical bed carved into a swan, with a large Louis Vuitton travel trunk at its foot. Ivory pillars of carved narwhal tusk supported the dressing table. The docent explained that after Major Dooley suffered a series of strokes, Sallie May had her niece move in with them to help.

The tour group viewed the other bedrooms, briefly inspected the butler's workspace, and then descended the stairs to exit the mansion. Upon exiting, the visitors found themselves gazing upon a statue of three women in a loving and intimate embrace in front of a reflecting pool. Much like the house and furnishings, which reflected the varied tastes, experiences, and travels of the Dooleys, the grounds and gardens also transported visitors to exotic lands. The statuary evoked a definite classical atmosphere, culminating with the mausoleum that held the remains of the Dooleys. While James Dooley had originally been buried with his Confederate comrades in Richmond's Hollywood Cemetery, he was later moved to rest with his wife in this classical tomb on the grounds of Maymont.

The girls toured the grounds together, remembering their many visits with their parents. After a long and exhausting walk, the girls went back to their car no closer to reaching the next step in their puzzle. They could see no tangible connection between the Dooleys, Maymont, and their mother.

Kate dropped her sister off at their home. Together, they planned to touch base later in the week to discuss next steps, as Kate wanted to get back to her own work. Their mother would be returning soon from her medical mission, and then they would all get together to catch up.

The girls were a bit disappointed to be stuck on the puzzle. Maybe Dad's plan wouldn't work out after all. Maybe he hadn't been able to complete his plan, due to his illness. "He did say he would send clues," Grace reminded her sister.

A few days later, the clue came: a birthday card, addressed to Kate and Grace from Beyond.

Grace trembled slightly as she opened the card. In it was a question:

When was Maymont added to the National Registry of Historic Places?

That was all it said.

Grace immediately ran a computer search. When she found the answer, she grinned and picked up the phone to dial her sister.

Kate answered her phone almost immediately. "I know the answer," Grace said brightly.

"What is it?" Kate said, her voice rising with excitement.

"Maymont was added to the National Registry of Historic Places in 1971," Grace said, hesitating for dramatic effect.

"Okay, so what?"

"On December sixteenth," Grace continued.

"Mom's birthday," said Kate.

The first puzzle was solved.

Chapter Nine

The Next Puzzle

"That was fun," Grace said.

The girls were in the kitchen of their childhood home. Although Grace still lived there, Kate was merely visiting, having rented a small apartment near her university downtown. Everyone had been surprised when Kate had moved. She had always said she hated the city. Still, she ultimately considered this house to be her home. After so many years spent growing up in these very rooms, it was a bit odd to feel somewhat like a visitor.

The pair was reviewing the "chain of evidence," as Kate had come to call the puzzle pieces:

Swannanoa, which was built by...

James and Sallie May Dooley, who had also built the Richmond landmark...

Maymont, which was added in 1971 to the National Registry of Historic Places on...

December 16, which was the birthday of...

Mom.

Grace had made lemonade, and was in the process of baking some cookies. As she looked at her sister, Kate couldn't help but be impressed. Grace was growing up. College suited her. She had done well, both academically and socially. Kate recalled her own first year in college: feeling both exhilarated and intimidated. But Grace had immediately made friends, as she always did. Sometimes, Kate admired the ease with which Grace interacted with people.

As Grace brought out the cookies she had baked, Kate went to their piano. She hadn't played for a while, and wondered how rusty she would be. As she sat down and began playing, however, she discovered she wasn't rusty at all. After a few notes, Chopin's Nocturne in C# minor began in earnest.

Music and the comforting smell of baking cookies wrapped around the girls like a blanket. Grace admired the fluidity of her sister's playing, though she was also an excellent pianist. For almost a decade, the girls had taken lessons from the same piano teacher, Miss Eunice, who had been an award-winning concert pianist in Korea, as well as a patient and kind teacher. Often, the girls' Friday Adventures with Dad had ended with treats in the Piano Café, the small coffee shop adjacent to the studio where the girls took piano lessons. There, the multitalented Miss Eunice also baked delicious cupcakes.

Kate came to a point in the song that she couldn't quite remember. "Bleh!" she exclaimed, as she stood up abruptly from the piano bench.

"That's one of my favorite pieces," Grace said gently.

"I don't get to play much anymore," Kate admitted. "I have access to some pianos at school, but I never use them. Since I'm not in the music program, it's almost like trespassing to use their facilities."

"You're always welcome to come here. I know Mom would love to listen to you play. So would I."

Kate blushed. She was touched by her sister's gentle invitation. Kate knew that she hadn't been around much recently. True, she had been busy with her work, but deep down, she knew that other things had kept her away from her home and family. She hated to admit it to herself, but the changes that had occurred after her father's death disturbed her greatly. Things just weren't the same. Routines that had been shaped over a lifetime had been lost. Things that were always a certain way no longer were. Kate accepted that as she aged, her life would change. That was natural, even welcome. But when her father had died, it was as if a solid touchstone was lost. It had been a year, almost to the day, since her dad had passed, and she still felt somehow unmoored. Yet at the same time, she felt silly for allowing herself to be affected in such a way. She had always prided herself on her mental toughness. Her discomfort, which she now realized sometimes felt like a weight on her chest, had caused her to retreat a bit from her family. There were times when she didn't want to be reminded of things, so she had worked, and worked, and worked some more.

She wondered if her mom was experiencing the same thing. A medical mission, while certainly noble, was not something she would have expected of her mother. People dealt with things in different ways, Kate supposed.

"Good cookies," Kate said as she munched a sugar cookie with toffee bits.

"Thanks!" Grace replied with obvious pleasure. She liked it when people honestly enjoyed her cooking.

Suddenly, Grace perked up as she heard a metallic click outside. "Oh, I think I hear the mailman. Let's see if we got anything today!"

She went outside for a moment. When she returned, she had a grin on her face. "We got another letter." She held another envelope, marked as before from Beyond.

Eagerly, the two girls opened the envelope and read.

My Sweet Girls,

I hope you had fun at Maymont. I trust that you figured this one out, once my clue arrived. I bet you're wondering how I am doing all of this, and all will be revealed at the end. But for now, I want to send you on your second mission. The same rules apply. Your second starting point is:

Loch Ness.

Enjoy,

Love,
Dad

Chapter Ten

Loch Ness

"You have to admit, Dad was a bit on the weird side," Kate said.

Grace had to nod. "He was certainly unique."

"So, Loch Ness and Mom, huh? And it can't be that she visited there."

Grace shook her head. "No. As I understand the rules, the connection to the Richmond landmark couldn't be that Mom had visited there, but he didn't say that restriction applied to other clues."

"Are you sure?" Kate asked, though she knew that Grace's memory and reasoning was likely correct. "Anyway, I don't think Mom has ever been to England."

"Scotland," Grace corrected. She quickly reached for her computer and typed for a few moments. "Loch Ness is near Inverness, in Scotland," she said.

"Well, Mom and I rode the Loch Ness Monster at Busch Gardens," Kate replied. Busch Gardens was one of the family's favorite vacation spots. They had visited the amusement park in Williamsburg,

Virginia, every year since the girls were little, until recently. Howl-O-Scream was a favorite event, when the park was decorated for Halloween with ghoulish characters that wandered the haunted grounds. Grace, however, distinctly remembered being terrified, and only grudgingly participating. She didn't really enjoy the rides that made her stomach flip, either. Grace's favorite place in the park had been the arcade. But she did enjoy the festive atmosphere, as well as the fact that everyone else seemed to have a good time.

"Should we go to Busch Gardens?" Kate asked.

"That's not really a Richmond thing," Grace replied. "Do you think he was referring to the real Loch Ness Monster?"

The girls thought for a moment. Their father, though a well-educated and fairly logical person, did have a fantastical streak in him. He even claimed to have seen an apparition once. Although the story may have changed some over the years, he resolutely reported seeing a bearded man, dressed in a Hawaiian shirt and visible only from the knees up, appear for a moment at the top of the stairs in their former home. He said that he was not frightened by the event, which he described as exactly that: "an event." Like witnessing a streak of lightning. For a moment, their dad had felt as if he could see into another place. He said he felt sure that the bearded man could see him as well, as a look of surprise had begun to form on the figure's face before it disappeared. Their dad stated that he went on about his business for a few seconds before he paused and said out loud, "What was that?" He claimed that their mother saw the same thing, but she wouldn't talk about it.

"Dad did like ghost stories and reading about the paranormal," Kate remembered. She shared her father's love of spooky stories, both reading and writing them. But as Kate thought further, she shook her head. Spooky stories were one thing, but the Loch Ness Monster myth and cryptozoology was something else. Kate was a scientist, whose worldviews were grounded in evidence-based research. She hoped to identify new insect species, and as such, knew that the proper scientific methodologies had to be applied for new knowledge to be considered valid. Although she didn't discount the possibility of new discoveries, when she was faced with what she considered pseudoscientific nonsense, her skeptical inclinations made her blood rise. She doubted that her father would have seriously entertained the Loch Ness Monster myth as real. And yet, he was the man who had a skull on his bookshelf and claimed to have seen an apparition.

She recalled a passage from one of her favorite books, *Discourse on the Method* by René Descartes. In this profound book from the history of philosophy and science, Descartes described his own intellectual development. He had studied what would now be called pseudoscience, feeling it a valid endeavor, even if it simply pointed out errors to avoid. Although Kate was no fan of mathematics (and Descartes was considered the father of analytic geometry), she thoroughly enjoyed reading about the history of science, especially Descartes. Cogito ergo sum.

Kate also knew that her father, like Descartes, was someone who held beliefs. He had said he believed in God, and had often gone to a Compline service at a church downtown. Kate had attended one of the services with him a few years ago. It had been thrilling, right up her dad's alley: held in virtual darkness, illuminated only with candlelight. Parishioners filed into the sanctuary in silence. The tang of incense filled the air. Then, at some unseen command, a single voice sang a line of verse. Soon thereafter, harmonious polyphony resonated throughout the church. When Kate had heard it for the first time, she felt a chill go up her spine and experienced a wave of emotion that she didn't expect, or even understand at the time.

"Wasn't that cool?" her dad had later asked her. She remembered nodding without speaking. "I like that kind of stuff," he had said. He paused and said, "God."

Sometimes, Kate's father had talked to his children

about spiritual things. Frequently, he talked about them in a booming voice that made him seem like he was kidding. Now, looking back on those times, Kate wondered if he had been speaking honestly, but in a way that wouldn't seem preachy or self-conscious.

Grace interrupted her musings. "I have to pick up Mom from the airport soon. Do you want to come?"

Kate had forgotten that their mother was due to return from Haiti later that day. She looked at her watch. "Sure," she said, thinking of the recent events, of which her mother was possibly—even likely— unaware. "Have we got a surprise for her!"

The girls' mother, Rebecca, had spent her adult life working as a nurse in cardiac intensive care, until she and her husband Kenneth had them. She had felt it important to be there for her children until they were school age.

Rebecca's father had worked two jobs to pay for her education, so she felt more than a little guilty when not working in her field. She and Kenneth both agreed that it was better for the girls if one of them was available on any given day. Rebecca eventually went back to work part-time. It was initially difficult for her to find a part-time nursing job. Her time away from nursing always seemed to work against her. But eventually, she found a position in the office practice of one of the physicians she knew from her days in the ICU. Luckily, Kenneth had been able to adjust his work schedule so that he was off when she worked, so the girls always had someone to care for them.

Rebecca's employer had always been supportive, especially after Kenneth became ill. After he had died, she had become active in the church where she grew up, St. Edward the Confessor Catholic Church. When her employer asked her to accompany his family on the medical mission to Haiti, and when her church's sister church in Haiti agreed to sponsor the trip, she had been thrilled. She wanted to give back.

The girls spent time with their mother, learning all about her trip, which had been exhausting, but satisfying. She had even had the opportunity to use her French language skills. During a lull in the conversation, Grace asked her mother, "Have you ever been to Scotland?"

"Scotland? No, why?"

The girls explained what had transpired. Rebecca was shocked. She told them she'd had no idea that their father had arranged the treasure hunt, and seemed a bit shaken. Kate and Grace saw unusual emotions pass across their mom's face as she took a moment to collect her thoughts.

"No. I've never been to Scotland," she said quietly,

suddenly pensive. Grace was unsure if her mom was experiencing sadness because she missed Dad, or because of something else.

"Dad was obviously thinking of you when he created this," Grace said gently.

"I wish he had told me about all of this. That's all."

Slowly a grin spread across Kate's face. "That may have spoiled the surprise. Besides, we'll share the treasure with you. After we find it!"

Chapter Eleven

Inverness

The girls decided to divide responsibilities in the search. Kate would look into the scientific and regional importance of Loch Ness; Grace would look into the monster legend. They decided to meet the following Friday for lunch. Then Kate left to return to her apartment, and Grace went to her room and began her research. Everyone had been surprised when Kate moved into an apartment downtown. She had always said she hated the city—but things change.

After an hour or so, she stopped. George Spicer, Hugh Gray, the Surgeon's Photograph, plesiosaurs, sonar mapping…yawn. Grace did not like monsters. For the first time since she and Kate had started the treasure hunt, she was bored. She felt as if they were off track somehow. There were no books on cryptozoology or other occult topics in her dad's library. There was no obvious connection between Mom and Loch Ness. Something was missing, and she was hungry. Time to bake some bread! She went to the kitchen and thought about the clues as she started the oven, and tried to reason out how her father was doing all this.

Kate, on the other hand, was in her element. Loch Ness was a large, deep freshwater lake in the Scottish Highlands twenty-three miles southwest of Inverness. The dark waters were murky due to the high peat content. Loch Ness contained more fresh water than all of the lakes of England and Wales combined, and it was the largest body of water on the Great Glen Fault, having formed there due to erosion along the fault zone during Quaternary glaciation. Work by Discovery Communications in 1993 had led to the discovery of a new nematode species and documentation of fish populations in Loch Ness previously unknown to science. Due to the depth of the loch, interesting disturbances known as seiches were visible via sonar when waters from different thermoclines interacted beneath the surface. Kate would love to kayak the loch! She would have to keep it in mind if she ever made it to Scotland.

As far back as she could remember, Kate had loved science and living things. She loved studying the natural world. Nature made sense to her. It was people she had a harder time understanding. Even the simple tyranny of having to say "Good morning!" with the proper amount of enthusiasm, lest one be thought rude, infuriated her.

Kate got on well with the members of her work team. Mara and her other work friends shared similar academic backgrounds and interest in science. Although each person was unique, they all shared a common focus on getting the work done that somehow made their social interactions less stressful. They had to interact and depend on one another to get the job done.

Kate was unsure whether they would be friends if they didn't have the commonality of their work. She supposed their group was similar to those found in many academic settings, or even other workplaces, for that matter: people formed relationships with those around them while they had to. Were these friendships deep or lasting? Perhaps, perhaps not; but as long as there was work, it didn't matter.

Kate's dad had once said that a true friend was someone you could call at 2:00 a.m. By that definition, Kate realized that Grace was not only her sister; she was also a true friend.

On Friday, the girls met for lunch at Bellytimber, one of their favorite restaurants. They had come there several times with their parents. The restaurant had excellent oven-fired pizzas. In a previous life, the place had been called the Texas-Wisconsin Border

Café and had been one of their dad's favorite haunts in his younger days. Their mom had lived in a small apartment not too far from the restaurant when she had attended college in town. That was one of the neat things about Richmond: although there was constant change, things also remained familiar.

The girls ordered the four-cheese pizza. While they waited, Kate asked, "Any progress on Loch Ness?"

Grace shook her head. "I can't see any connections to Mom. You?"

Kate also shook her head. "It's an interesting area, but I can't really see any connections to Mom either. I spoke with her last night, and neither of us could see where Dad was going with this."

The food arrived, and the girls munched on the crispy, thin-crust pizza.

"Did you decide what you're going to do for the summer?" Kate asked.

Grace thought for a moment. "I was thinking about working at Rita's again, but I haven't made any arrangements yet. I should call soon." She paused. "Although, after all of this business," she said, referring to their fanciful treasure hunt, "I'm not sure I want to. I may want to stay free in case we get any more letters."

Kate nodded. She approved of her sister's work

ethic, although she knew that, given her sister's frugality and their dad's insurance money, Grace didn't have to work if she didn't want to. Their education was paid for. Their living finances were secure. Their parents had been determined in their preparations.

"What do you think he was trying to do with all of this?" Grace asked.

Kate started to grin. "I know exactly what he was trying to do. I think he wanted to have fun." Her smile faded a bit as she continued. "I think he knew his time was coming to an end. I think he planned this as a way to have fun during the last weeks, when he had such trouble. I bet he smiled when he thought about this unfolding after he was gone." Grace nodded solemnly. "I wonder why he waited a year to start?"

Without hesitation, Grace replied, "Out of respect for us. It wouldn't have been fun right after. I think he knew we would need time." She said this with conviction, and it was obvious to both of the girls that this was true.

Kate looked at her sister and thought—this girl is smart.

They finished their pizza and went their separate ways. As she entered her apartment, Kate heard the phone ring.

"Hello?"

Her sister's voice came through the speaker. "We

got another letter!" she exclaimed, with obvious excitement.

"What's it say?" Kate asked.

Grace read:

My Sweet Girls,
Do you need a clue?
Here it is:
"Who was King of Inverness in
1040?"

The letter was unsigned.

"That doesn't help," Kate said after a pause.

"Give me a moment," Grace said. She picked up her handheld computer and typed a few words. "The king of Inverness—in fact, of all of Scotland—in 1040 was King Mac Bethad mac Findlaich."

"I have no idea who that is," Kate said.

"Yes, you do," Grace replied. "You just know him by his more famous nickname."

"Which is?"

"Macbeth."

"Macbeth, as in Shakespeare?" Kate asked.

"The same," Grace answered.

Both girls knew in an instant where this was leading. They both said simultaneously—

"Agecroft."

Chapter Twelve

The Scottish Play

"Let's get this straight right up front: we are not the Weird Sisters!" Kate said with indignation. Grace agreed.

The girls had decided to get together to read through *Macbeth*. Grace insisted on calling it "the Scottish Play."

"Why?" Kate had asked.

"Theatrical tradition!" Grace had said, pointing her index finger in the air. "And maybe a curse, too, but I doubt that part."

"What the—?" Kate said, with an incredulous look.

Grace explained that, according to theatrical lore, it was unlucky to say the word "Macbeth" in a theatre. If someone did, he would have to leave the theatre, go outside, spin around three times, spit or curse, and then ask to be let back into the theatre, as a way to ward off bad luck.

Legend had it that the play was cursed. Shakespeare had written it during the time of King James I of England (formerly James VI of Scotland). King James, who had sponsored the official King James version of the Bible in 1604, was a learned man who had written a book on the detection of and fight against witchcraft. In fact, in 1590, he had been personally involved in one of the first witch trials in North Berwick, Scotland, which had ended with the execution of an admitted witch (whose confession was obtained via torture). To put this into historical perspective, Jamestown (also named for the king) had been founded in 1607, and the first Salem witch trials held in 1692. But during the long reign of James I, also known as the Jacobean Period (which followed the Elizabethan Age), the golden age of Shakespearean theater thrived. And what better way to catch the attention of your richest and most powerful patron than by starting a play with something about which the king himself had such deep and personal knowledge?

It was whispered that Shakespeare had written actual incantations into the Weird Sisters' dialogue in *Macbeth*, which may have led to the play being cursed. This legend was a bit different from other theater legends, such as not whistling in a theatre. That lore had grown out of the fact that Shakespearean theatrical productions often used out-of-work sailors to man the heights above the stage, lowering scenery or props, often at the direction of a whistle. If a sailor in the rafters heard a stray whistle, he might accidentally lower a heavy prop that could injure actors on the stage. Actors, not unlike baseball players, have developed many legends (and some superstitions) surrounding their craft. The Macbeth legend is one such example.

The girls read through the play. It was one of the shortest plays in the Shakespeare canon, and it was dark. War, dark magic, betrayal, bloody murder, regicide, infanticide, and madness filled his powerful tragedy. The language took a little getting used to. Many lines had to be read and reread to glean the meaning. But the language had undeniable power. This guy could write. Allusions to clothing, which seemed odd at first, helped weave the narrative of a man who began the play as a hero whose clothes fit him well, but who descended into being a monster, hardly recognizable in his ill-fitting clothes. At the end of the play, he became the very thing he had destroyed at the beginning. Although Macbeth's ambition seemed to have been the driving force of the play, ambition alone did not quite fully explain the inexorable transformation in Macbeth. Perhaps Shakespeare did indeed hint at darker forces within human nature, or at least darker forces to which some are susceptible. One thing was certain: this play had impact.

And it was meant to be viewed as a performance. Although Shakespeare's works were now some of the most widely published writings in Western literature along with the Bible and the works of Agatha Christie, his plays were meant to be viewed, not read. Shakespeare had worked in an age when copyright law was just developing, and there were actually several versions of some of his most famous plays. During his most active period, Shakespeare and his company, called the King's Men since they were sponsored by King James I starting in 1603, produced on average twelve plays per year. The sheer volume of work, many or most or all of which were now considered masterpieces of genius, spoke to a unique set of circumstances that allowed this living art to be created. Four hundred years after their creation, they still moved people. Despite the plays' archaic language and circumstances, modern readers and playgoers could still identify with characters with odd names like Banquo or Donalbain.

Though the girls had read the play, they hadn't seen it in production. After watching some excellent video versions of the Scottish Play, the girls wanted to see a live performance. And there was only one place that would serve: the Richmond Shakespeare Festival at Agecroft Hall.

Chapter Thirteen

Agecroft

For decades, the Richmond Shakespeare Company had produced the bard's plays outdoors in the courtyard of Agecroft Hall. The troupe had gone through different iterations over the years, merging with other theatrical groups such as the Henley Street Theatre Company; and every summer, the company held a traditional Shakespeare festival.

The girls were not surprised that their father had included Shakespeare in one of his clues: during his final years, he had become quite a Shakespeare enthusiast, and they knew he always looked forward to the productions. They had gone with him to a few plays over the years, but never one of Shakespeare's tragedies.

Unfortunately, *Macbeth* was not on the menu for this season, so the girls went to see *Othello*. They arrived in the evening, as the heat of the summer day was starting to recede, and the sounds of insects gradually increased as a crowd began to gather on the lawns before Agecroft Hall.

The stately dwelling overlooked the James River, perched on a rolling grassy hill of landscaped grounds including an Elizabethan knot garden, a bowling green, a maze, a sunken garden with fountain and statuary, lush boxwoods surrounding a stillhouse, and a large courtyard.

The house itself was just as impressive. It had begun its life in England as the manor house of the Prestwich family after 1292, when Edmund Crouchback, Earl of Lancaster, granted land near the Irwell River in Lancashire County to Adam de Prestwich. In 1350, one of the female Prestwich heirs, Johanna de Tetlow, married Richard de Langley after her family died from infection (possibly the plague). The Langleys, a prominent local family who made money off of their land as wool merchants, lived at the hall until their male line ended in 1561. They adopted the name Agecroft circa 1376, from the terms "ache" (pronounced like the letter H, meaning "wild celery") and "croft," meaning "field." Over time, "Ache-Croft" became "Agecroft."

In 1925, Thomas C. Williams transported the large Tudor structure to the United States after purchasing it at auction in England. He painstakingly had the home, which had fallen into disrepair and was being considered for demolition, disassembled and shipped to Richmond. Winston Churchill, Britain's Home Secretary and Chancellor of the Exchequer at the time, had become personally involved in determining the legality of the purchase and overseeing transport of the historic house to the US.

Even before its move to Richmond, Agecroft Hall had had several historic Shakespearean connections. The first Robert Langley had been a ward of John of Gaunt, who, in addition to being one of the wealthiest men in history (some estimates put his comparable adjusted wealth in the $110 billion range, the sixteenth richest person in the history of the world), was a friend and relative of Chaucer, as well as a Shakespearean character. In his famous speech in *Richard II*, he describes his homeland as "This blessed plot, this earth, this realm, this England." He was born in Ghent, which became known as Gaunt, to King Edward III and Phillipa of Hainault. He was the first Duke of Lancaster of the House of Plantagenet, and the younger brother of Edward, the Black Prince of Wales. He became a pivotal figure in European history: although he himself never ruled England, he was heir to three of the great ruling houses of Britain, and his children by his three wives became the sovereign rulers of England as heads of the houses of Lancaster, York, and Tudor.

Kate and Grace made their way across the lawn toward the courtyard, which had been supplied with stadium seating that faced a platform that would serve as the stage for the evening's performance of *Othello*. Strolling minstrels sang and played Renaissance music as the festive atmosphere of the impending performance took hold. While waiting for the audience to be seated, a small group of young actors in period dress approached the line of patrons and asked, "Good morrow, gentle folk. Wouldst thou like to hear a speech from *Henry V*?" Kate and Grace both grinned and said yes, and the troupe immediately launched into the St. Crispin's Day speech. After the rousing rendition, the group bowed and moved to another cluster of waiting patrons.

Grace thrilled at the pomp and ceremony. There was a magical quality to theater that she had always loved. Not only could theater transport you to a different time and place, but live performances created their own reality in which one could exist for a time. Grace thought of the times that her father had toured the house and gardens with her, both on Friday Adventures and on school field trips. Most visits to Agecroft focused on the beauty or history of the house. This was different. This trip was an event. It was a moment in time when a group of interested and knowledgeable people came together in the spirit of comity to share an experience. It was wonderful.

But the bills had to be paid. Before the performance, a group of performers explained that a treasure chest would be present at the end of the play so that "appreciation"—meaning funds—could be shared with the actors. Grace knew from her study of the theater that practical issues such as funding had always been a concern for the producers of this unique art. In Shakespeare's time, actors were often not held in esteem, and acting troupes were often under the protection of a powerful sponsor or risked arrest as vagrants. That was why Shakespeare's troupe was called the Lord Chamberlain's Men, and then the King's Men under James I. The names clearly conveyed that the group was under the protection and patronage of the king. As such, Shakespeare was in a favored position, and was able to experiment with ways to improve his cash flow. Out of these experiments grew the concepts of the theatrical venue, and controlled admission to a finite group of paying audience members. Shakespeare's venues were the Rose and Globe Theatres. These developments, along with the development of copyright law, helped preserve the integrity of the troupe's performances and secure income for their productions.

The sun went down as the gentle summer night embraced the estate, and the play began. Kate and

Grace watched as it told the tragedy of the noble Moor Othello and his manipulation by Iago, to the ruin of his marriage and the death of both Othello and his faithful wife, Desdemona. Although the girls struggled initially with the language, once the play hit its stride, they understood most of what was happening, especially the subtle maneuverings of Iago. By the time the treasure chest was displayed as the crowd filed out past the assembled actors, the girls were emotionally spent. They lingered a while on the front lawn, not quite wanting the evening to be over. Cicadas had started to buzz, a sure sign that the summer would soon start to fade. Both girls felt that familiar pang in their stomachs that they always experienced when they knew a new school year would soon be approaching.

They decided to go to a local restaurant not far away. They parked in a small lot on Cary Street in Carytown, a prominent and well-established shopping area that had long been fashionable, especially for students and young professionals. Over the years, the girls had taken a series of writing classes at a local bookstore in the area. Kate and Grace both had copyrighted works on their resumes, and both were proud of their creative endeavors.

They walked a short way from the parking lot to the entrance of Can Can, a French-themed brasserie that they had visited many times, and which had changed very little over the years. The French décor added to the festive atmosphere, and Kate could remember many visits with their dad, munching on cheese and wonderful bread with lots of butter as they talked about books or stories or museums they had just visited.

They went in and sat on their usual stools at the bar. The counter was metal, comfortably worn. Kate considered ordering wine, but Grace was still under the legal drinking age, so instead, she ordered fizzy water with lime. Grace did the same. They ordered a cheese plate, which featured several types of cheese, a meat pâté, and olives, and which was one of Kate's favorite dishes, to share.

Grace spread some Brie onto a crispy toasted cracker. She tried one of the olives and made a face. "Nope. I still don't get it," she said. Their father had loved olives from the cheese plate, as well as the raw oysters the restaurant offered. Grace felt that it was indeed a brave man who had first tried raw oysters, while Kate, who was (mostly) vegetarian, was simply horrified whenever her dad ate seafood.

"Did you enjoy the play?" Grace asked.

"I hate it when people ask me if I like stuff!" was Kate's almost reflexive reply. Grace grinned, knowing how Kate would react.

"I thought they did a really good job," Grace

offered. "Did you notice how they had a background of low-pitched vibration behind the audience during dramatic scenes?" Kate shook her head. "It was more something you felt rather than heard," Grace explained. "It seemed to heighten the dread."

Grace had been studying artistic production and performance. Since she was little, she had always said that she wanted to make movies. Initially it had, perhaps, been a fanciful desire, but now that she was in college, she was seriously considering the arts as a career choice. She had always loved reading and writing. She was not afraid of public performance and had performed as a pianist and in school plays during her academic career. She had considered pursuing drama in her first year of college, but given the circumstances, she had decided to hunker down and just get through her academic classes as best she could. Perhaps it was time to reconsider.

Chapter Fourteen

The Shakespearean Clue

Grace woke up with a start. She had been dreaming. She was usually a very sound sleeper. Maybe it was the cheese. Or a bit of underdone potato, she thought to herself, with a little Dickens.

Her dream had not been frightening, but she clearly remembered seeing him—not as he was in the end, sick and drawn, but vigorous and young. He had smiled, but nothing more. She felt comforted.

Now she was fully awake, and went downstairs. Mom had gone to the grocery store, a note on the counter said. Her mom was typically an early riser who liked to get things done. Grace made herself some hot tea— "Early Grey," as she liked to call it. She took the tea up to her dad's office and sat in his leather chair. Their old cat, Saucy, had used it as a claw sharpener, much to Dad's chagrin. Grace curled her legs up and hugged her knees as she sipped the tea. She felt it. Something was going to happen today.

Later that day, the mail came.

Kate answered her phone. "Hello?"

"We got another clue today," Grace stated.

"What's it say?"

Grace read:

> "Act IV, scene 3: Who was canonized by Pope Alexander III in 1161?"

"Is that it?"

"No," Grace said. "The clue was written in a card."

"What type of card?"

"'Congratulations on Your Baptism.'"

"Wait a minute." Grace heard Kate shuffling papers. "I bought an old copy of the Scottish Play. A Penguin Classic! It smells like Chop Suey," Kate said, referring to the used bookstore where the girls had taken writing classes. That shop was always full of the wonderful smell of old books, as well as Won Ton, the old cat who often slept in the store's sunny front window.

"Act IV." Grace heard the turning of pages. "Scene 1, witches. Scene 2—oh, yuck—the family MacDuff. Scene 3. Here it is." Kate paused as she read.

"What's it about?" Grace asked after a few seconds.

"Malcolm and MacDuff, Malcolm and MacDuff, Malcolm and Ross and MacDuff; a doctor who exits."

"That's it?"

"That's about it."

Grace looked at the clue. "Who was canonized? Doesn't that mean 'made into a saint'?"

"Yes. I don't think any of these guys were saints." Kate looked at the footnotes in her Penguin Classic. "Wait a minute. I think I have it!" Grace heard Kate scribbling on paper. "This scene takes place in England. At the court of King Edward."

"Okay."

"King Edward the Confessor."

"Okay."

"Do you have your computer handy?"

Grace was already at work. "That's it," she said. "He was canonized in 1161 by Pope Alexander III as Saint Edward the Confessor."

"Whose namesake church was where Mom was baptized."

Grace said, "So, the chain of evidence goes like this:

Loch Ness, which is in Scotland near...

Inverness, which was ruled in 1040 by...

King Macbeth, whose rule was fictionalized by...

William Shakespeare, whose plays are performed at the Richmond landmark...

Agecroft Hall, by the Richmond Shakespeare Company, who has performed the play...

Macbeth, which takes place, in Act IV, scene 3, at the court of...

Edward the Confessor, who was canonized in 1161 as...

St. Edward the Confessor, who became the patron and namesake of...

St. Edward Catholic Church, in Richmond, Virginia, where was baptized...

Mom

The girls took a deep breath. The second puzzle was done.

Chapter Fifteen

The Last Puzzle

The note read:

> Dearest Kate and Grace,
> I hope you enjoyed Agecroft. That place was always one of my favorites. Are you ready for your last puzzle? Here we go. Your final starting point is: The Old Stone House.
> Proceed with caution.
> Dad

"That's kind of ominous," Kate said with a sly smile. This was a private joke between the two.

Grace said, "The Old Stone House. That rings a bell."

Kate nodded on the video screen. Grace had

called Kate as soon as she had received another letter. Weeks had passed since they began the Adventure. The summer was winding down. Soon school would be back in session. They both wanted to find the treasure before school started again.

Grace had already typed a few lines into her computer. She nodded firmly. "I thought so. The Old Stone House is the site of the Poe Museum."

"So this puzzle virtually begins with the Richmond landmark," Kate replied. "Now we need to connect the Poe Museum or Poe to Mom."

Grace had a look of distaste on her face. "Poe was weird," she said. She had never really liked Poe's macabre writing. The only thing that she liked from Poe was the poem "El Dorado." That poem, although a bit melancholy, at least had a peppy rhythm. She remembered her father reading "The Tell-Tale Heart" to them in one of the upstairs rooms of the museum on one of their Friday Adventures. Her dad had loved creepy stuff. He had read the poem with theatrical flair, and she had been both thrilled and a bit uneasy, not knowing what would happen next. In the end, she had come away from the experience wide-eyed and unnerved.

As for the Poe Museum, the family had gone there many times. Once, one of the changing exhibit galleries had housed a gruesome tableau recreated from "The Pit and the Pendulum," complete with Halloween props that were quite frightening. Just as with Howl-O-Scream, Grace didn't really like to be frightened. She liked her life to run gently and smoothly, with no loud noises or sudden shocks.

Kate had to agree on Poe. "Yes, he was a bit on the strange side. I see why Dad liked him."

"How do you want to do this?" Grace asked. Kate thought for moment.

"You know, I really don't know that much about Poe. You would think that we would, since he had Richmond connections, but I really don't," Kate admitted. "Let's research the man and see if any connections come up."

Grace agreed.

"Do you think we should read some of his works?" Kate asked.

Grace made a face. "I don't think I'm up to any gut-wrenching horror at this moment."

Kate smiled. "Okay, how about his detective stories?"

"What do you mean?"

"Poe wrote some detective stories."

"Like Sherlock Holmes?" Grace asked.

"Before Sherlock Holmes," Kate replied. "If I remember correctly, Poe wrote the first detective stories ever written. Some say his detective was the forerunner of Sherlock Holmes."

Grace was still unsure, but said, "That doesn't sound too bad. Do you want to come over and read together?" The girls had frequently read together growing up. The quiet companionship was familiar and comforting.

Kate grinned. "How about some pull-apart bread and you've got a deal!"

The girls decided to read the three stories featuring Poe's detective, C. Auguste Dupin. They started with "The Murders in the Rue Morgue." Kate had never read Poe's detective stories before, and she had to admit she was impressed. In the stories, Poe described a line of reasoning not unlike the chain of evidence the girls were following in solving their own puzzles. But what caught Kate's attention, along with Poe's skill with language both modern and classical, was the knowledge he exhibited of the science of his day—evidence of his wide-ranging intellect. He most notably mentioned one of Kate's favorites from the history of science: Georges Cuvier, a French naturalist and zoologist who had helped expand on the taxonomy of living creatures and binomial nomenclature developed by Carl Linnaeus, and whose importance to science was reflected by his name being one of those inscribed on the Eiffel Tower.

Far from being lurid or overly infatuated with the violence of murder, Poe's detective stories seemed familiar. Their protagonist, Dupin, was a brilliant but slightly odd detective who was not a policeman, but a private citizen who thrilled in the intellectual exercises that detection offered. Dupin had a faithful companion who acted as the story's narrator, and there was a police official who consulted Dupin on particularly puzzling cases. The parallel to Holmes and Watson was remarkable.

In the three short stories featuring Dupin— "The Murders in the Rue Morgue," "The Mystery of Marie Roget," and "The Purloined Letter" —Poe set the familiar pattern that many future detective and mystery stories would follow. As a testament to the fact that Poe was the first mystery writer, the Edgar Allan Poe Awards (or simply, the Edgars) had been awarded every year by the Mystery Writers of America to writers in the detective and mystery genre since the 1940s.

After reading the three short mysteries, the girls thumbed through some of Poe's poetry.

"He writes a lot about death," Grace noted.

Kate nodded as she reached for some of Grace's homemade pull-apart bread. This was one of Nannie's recipes from the spice rack.

"What do you think happens when you die?"

Grace asked. Kate stopped chewing.

"Wow. That's a big question," she answered. She knew better than to give the namby-pamby "What do you think?" reply. She hated it when adults who didn't know any answers threw this response to kids— although, looking at her sister, she knew Grace wasn't a kid. And Grace was smart, smart enough to have asked the question in sincere hope of a real response.

Kate thought for a moment, then replied, "My training in biology leads me to say that once the brain of an organism is dead, whatever made that living thing an individual ceases to be, the body decays, and the person is gone."

Grace nodded grimly. "That seems logical. Do you think that's what Dad believed?"

Kate hesitated. "I heard him say that he feared that we wink out of existence at death. If that's the case, then life is a peculiarity, since there'd be an eternity before we exist and an eternity after we exist, and just a short time that we do exist as individuals on Earth." Kate looked with tenderness at her sister. She knew that Grace was a sensitive and caring person. "But to be honest, I don't know what happens to us at death. No one does. But I do think that Dad was a spiritual person. He held beliefs in God, and even though he wondered about winking out of existence, I don't know if that's what he believed. I also heard him tell

Mom that they would see each other again one day."

Grace seemed thoughtful. "People don't seem to talk a lot about sickness or death," she said.

Kate nodded. "That's true. I suspect that most people are afraid of it, and to speak of it makes it seem more real and frightening."

Grace continued. "I suspect that Poe's morbid writing reflects his own experiences with grief. Until you experience loss yourself, it is hard to really understand what it feels like. I see that in Poe." Grace stood up with a look of resolve. "I want us to go to the Poe house," she said.

Kate looked at her sister and nodded. "Okay," she said—then added, "Commander."

Chapter Sixteen

The Old Stone House

They parked off Main Street, near the Holocaust Museum.

"We should go there sometime," Kate said.

They looked down Main Street, toward the farmers' market. When the traffic allowed, they crossed Main and headed toward an old stone house that seemed oddly out of place among the shops and restaurants that surrounded it. Next to the house was a peaceful-looking courtyard surrounded by an iron fence and stone pillars. On the ground among the bricks was a marker stating that this was one of the stops on the Historic Richmond Tour.

The house's door looked old and worn. The knob, made of brass, was oddly small. A placard advertised a ghost walk for that evening.

This was the Poe Museum.

Unlike Poe shrines in other towns that lay claim to some part of the life of the renowned writer, like

Boston, Baltimore, Philadelphia, and New York, Poe had never lived or worked in this building. The Old Stone House was simply said to be the oldest extant house in Richmond. During the Civil War and at other times, during other tragedies, most of Richmond had burned or been otherwise destroyed. But the Old Stone House had remained, steadfast. Next to its door was a plaque that read:

The Oldest House
Still Standing in Richmond
Probably built 1737 by Jacob Ege
A gift in 1912 from
Mr. and Mrs. Granville G. Valentine
to the Association for the
Preservation of Virginia Antiquities
Restored by Mr. And Mrs. Archer G. Jones
In 1924 placed in custody of the
Edgar Allan Poe Shrine (now the
Edgar Allan Poe Foundation, INC.)

The house did have a Colonial look to it. It would have blended nicely into the row of houses on Duke of Gloucester Street in Colonial Williamsburg.

The girls entered the front room of the house, which had been converted into a gift shop where visitors paid (or in the girls' case, where members registered) to enter the museum. The museum itself was not a single building, but rather a series of buildings surrounding a lovely and peaceful garden large enough for an intimate gathering, and indeed, many weddings had been held there over the years. At the far end of the garden was an alcove with a bust of Poe, while in the other buildings were displayed many artifacts from Poe's time in Richmond.

Poe had spent a large part of his life in Richmond, and had at one point considered himself a Virginian. But he had been born in Boston, on January 19, 1809, to actors David Poe and Elizabeth Arnold Hopkins Poe. Edgar may have been named for a character in King Lear, the play the two actors were performing in 1809. He had two siblings: an older brother, William Henry Leonard Poe; and a younger sister, Rosalie. Poe's father, David Poe Jr., was son of David Poe Sr., who had been a much-beloved quartermaster in the American Revolution. The junior Poe defied his father's wish for him to become a lawyer and had gone into theater. It was generally believed that David Poe was a mediocre actor, especially when compared with his more acclaimed wife, and it was also suggested that he exhibited an ill temper and struggled with alcohol.

Edgar Poe's early life had started poorly, when David Poe abandoned the family in 1810. Edgar then lost his mother to tuberculosis in 1811. She was buried in the church graveyard of St. John's Church on Richmond's Church Hill, the same church where Patrick Henry gave his famous "Give Me Liberty or Give Me Death!" speech. Whether one believed in fate or not, Poe's earliest years seemed to foreshadow a pattern in his life: conflict with male authority figures, loss of important females, struggles with alcohol, and love of the arts, the last of which played a significant role in the disposition of the Poe children after Eliza's death. The prominent Richmond businessman John Allan, along with his wife, Frances, was an avid supporter of the theater. Indeed, as Eliza Poe grew ill, several Richmond ladies, including Frances Allan, helped care for her. After Eliza's death, the Allans assumed the responsibility of arranging care for her orphans.

All these facts and more were relayed to the girls at the registration counter by Emily, the volunteer who handed them laminated information sheets. Grace couldn't help but like Emily's "emo" style: black hair tinted with purple, dark eyeliner, and pale skin.

Before they left to tour the museum, the girls looked around the gift shop. It smelled old, and the bare wooden plank floor creaked in places. A closed door constructed beneath a staircase to the left of the checkout register led to a room containing the first of the Poe artifacts. The doorframe seemed small, though the room, which would have been a sitting area when the museum was still a private residence, was of a decent size, with a sizeable stone hearth.

The shop's merchandise certainly tended toward the gruesome: candy lollipops shaped like red hearts, black cats, gold bugs, pictures and busts of Poe, and, of course, ravens. "The Raven," Poe's most famous work and, one could argue, the piece that had made his name in the literary world, had sold for only a few dollars. Poe had been one of the first writers to try to make a living from his literary work, but despite his now-acknowledged genius and his impressive output, he struggled financially for most of his life.

In addition to what Emily told them, the girls had done their own homework on Poe, and they were anxious to learn more. But for some reason, they were both just a bit apprehensive. Hesitating for a split second, they entered the museum through the small door beneath the staircase.

Displayed in this room were artifacts from Poe's early life. Poe's boyhood bed was there, donated by the Raven Society of the University of Virginia. The girls knew that Poe had been in the university's second entering class. His focus had been languages, for which he evidently had an aptitude. However, due to financial pressures, he left the university after one year. Despite his not graduating, the University of Virginia still claimed Poe as an alumnus.

Displays in this room remarked on the fact that Poe had been athletic—surprising Kate, who had always pictured Poe as sickly. In fact, in his youth, Poe had been a participant in track and field as well as boxing, and it was also claimed that he had swum six miles in the James River—claimed. There seemed to be several claims about Poe's life and work that raised eyebrows. He was a complicated man.

The room also held Rosalie Poe's piano. Edgar's younger sister Rosalie had lived most of her life under the care of Jane Scott Mackenzie, who had been a friend of Poe's guardian, Francis Allan. Rosalie eventually taught penmanship at Mackenzie's school. She was also supported by selling portraits of her famous brother, and by charity: Joseph Gallego, whose wife Mary had lived at Poe's childhood home of Moldavia, and who perished in the Richmond Theatre fire in 1811, gave Rosalie Poe two thousand dollars in his will. The theatre fire had been a tremendous event in Richmond's history. The fire killed seventy-two people, including the sitting Virginia governor, George William Smith. At the time, it was the worst urban disaster in American history.

The girls soon learned that the tragic fire had occurred on December 26, 1811, at the Richmond Theatre on the north side of Broad Street between 12th and College. The Richmond Theatre had been a prominent part of Richmond's cultural life since its opening on October 12, 1786. Originally proposed as an academy of fine arts and sciences by Chevalier Quesney de Beaurepaire, a French officer who had served in the American Revolutionary War, the Richmond Theatre was the site of the Virginia Ratifying Convention in 1788. James Madison, John Marshall, James Monroe, Edmund Pendleton, George Wythe, George Nicholas, Edmond Randolph, George Mason, Richard Henry Lee, and Patrick Henry had all attended.

On the night of December 26, 1811, the Richmond Theatre was filled with 598 people attending a benefit for Richmond citizen Alexander Placide and his daughter. The play had originally been scheduled for December 23, but had been postponed until after Christmas due to the death of Eliza Poe (along with the illness of Placide, combined with bad weather). On the bill were The Father (or, Family Feuds) and Raymond Agnes (or, The Bleeding Nun). As the curtain fell after the first act, (which play?) one of the chandeliers was raised. It became entangled in the ropes used to hoist it up, and the lit candles came into contact with some of the dozens of scenery screens that could be lowered during a performance. Like falling dominoes, they all began to burn. The fire quickly spread to the pine rafters of the roof. Since the stage curtain was down, the audience did not know of the danger until it was upon them. Panic ensued. Many were trampled as they tried to escape. Only the heroic efforts of many, including a freed slave named Gilbert Hunt, who helped dozens escape through a window, kept the death toll from being worse.

In the end, fifty-four women and eighteen men perished in the fire. Their remains were memorialized on the site, and remained there under the structure of Monumental Church, an Episcopal church commissioned by Chief Justice John Marshall and built between 1812 and 1814. Robert Mills, the only architectural student of Thomas Jefferson, had designed the building, as well as the Washington Monument and the White House of the Confederacy. As long-time Richmond residents, John Marshall and his family occupied pew number twenty-three in the new church. The Allans, along with Edgar Poe, sat in pew number eighty. In 1965, the church was deconsecrated and given by the Medical College of Virginia to the Historic Richmond Foundation, an affiliate of the Association for the Preservation of Virginia Antiquities.

After looking at the portraits of John and Francis Allan, Mrs. Mackenzie, Mary Gallego, and Rosalie, as well as a portrait of Edgar Allan Poe that hung over the fireplace, Kate and Grace returned to the gift shop. Emily smiled and nodded to another door at the rear of the gift shop that led to the rectangular Enchanted Garden, which was surprisingly serene. Outside, a brick path surrounded a grassy area lined by small shrubs, with a water fountain at the far end of the garden, before an alcove housing a bust of Poe. Iron benches provided a peaceful place to watch the birds that splashed in the fountain reservoir.

From the garden, another door led into a separate building: the Model Building. In this room was a large-scale model of Richmond as it had appeared in the time of Poe. The Model Building also held artifacts that showcased Poe as artist, author, and critic.

During his life, Poe had been friendly with painter Robert Sully and illustrator Felix Darley. One of the Model Building's exhibits showed a drawing, supposedly by Poe himself, of a woman weeping after reading a letter that had fallen to the floor at her feet. The building also housed artifacts such as Poe's desk and furniture from his days as a journalist and literary critic at the Southern Literary Messenger, where Poe made a name for himself as a (sometimes harsh) literary critic. One literary piece so disappointed Poe that he suggested that the author shoot himself.

The furniture from the Southern Literary Messenger was also a bit odd. Poe's publisher, Thomas

Willis White, who now rested in the cemetery of St. John's Church along with Poe's mother, had had the back of Poe's chair cut low so that Poe "would have to sit up straight." It seemed that many people in Poe's life had wanted to parent him.

Other exhibits in the Model Building told of Poe's life as a soldier, which came as another surprising revelation regarding Poe who had left the University of Virginia after his not-quite-adoptive father, John Allan, rejected his plea for funds. After leaving the university, Poe enlisted in the U.S. Army. Many of the turning points in Poe's life seemed to come after conflicts with Allan, with whom he apparently did not get along.

Poe had served, evidently with distinction, as an artificer—one who mixes gunpowder and explosives. He used the locations of his postings, such as Moultrie, South Carolina, as settings for his stories, such as "The Gold Bug." He later left the army after agreeing to pay (and then evidently not paying) someone to take his place—this being a not uncommon practice of the time. Poe was then accepted into West Point Military Academy, as he attempted to become an officer, and again excelled in languages. He left after just one year, expelled for dereliction of duty. Moment after moment of Poe's life seemed to reflect the pattern of his early childhood: conflict with authority, financial struggles, and grandiose plans, with little accomplishment aside from his writing.

The girls left the Model Building and walked across the Enchanted Garden to the Memorial Building, whose main room was dominated by a classical-style carved marble memorial created by Richard Henry Park. Edwin Booth and the Actors of New York had commissioned the memorial, which showed a woman in classical drapery placing a garland around a relief carving of the bust of Edgar Allan Poe. The memorial read:

> *This Memorial, expressing a deep and personal sympathy between the Stage and the Literature of America, was placed here by the Actors of New York, to commemorate the American poet Edgar Allan Poe—whose parents, David Poe, Jr. and Elizabeth Arnold, his wife—were Actors, and whose renown should, therefore, be cherished, with peculiar reverence and pride, by the Dramatic Profession of his country. He was born in Boston, the 19th of January, 1809; he died in Baltimore, the 7th of October, 1849. He was great in his genius; unhappy in his life; wretched in his death. But in his fame he is immortal.*

Together, the girls looked at the other artifacts in the room. There was the trunk whose key had been found in Poe's pocket after his death, and a lock of Poe's hair. There was a small display of some of the early copies of "The Murders in the Rue Morgue," along with descriptions of Poe's impact on detective fiction.

The girls quickly left the Memorial Building and walked across a smaller courtyard to the Exhibit Building, which held rotating displays of Poe-related artifacts. At various times, this room had featured exhibits on Poe in film, Poe's influence around the world, the women in the life of Poe, and now, the impact of Poe on science fiction. Kate was surprised and delighted to find that Poe had written an original foreword to a book on the classification of seashells—his bestselling and most profitable venture in his own lifetime. In addition to pioneering work in detective fiction, Poe had written what would now be considered science fiction. His tales of reanimation and mummy-unwrapping parties reflected the fascination with Egypt that had been popular in his time—the same Egypt mania made evident in the Egyptian Building that had been constructed on the campus of the Medical College of Virginia in 1845. In addition, Poe had written of air travel, space travel, the universe, mesmerism, and exploration. The discovery of Antarctica in 1820 had led to Poe's only novel, *The Narrative of Arthur Gordon Pym.*

The girls went upstairs. At the top of the stairs was a small landing. Period furniture rested in the hallway.

On the walls hung artwork inspired by themes from Poe's works. There were several representations of ravens, of course, but also other works.

Grace went over to a painting depicting a naked Tahitian girl on a bed. Behind the bed, people seemed to be walking, not noticing the girl. As one's eyes moved from the girl in the uncomfortable presence of fully clothed passersby (Were they strangers, and did they see her?), one could see the word "Nevermore" in the upper left of the painting, as if it were on a poster. In the window next to the Nevermore poster stood a bird. Awkwardly looking at the girl (or the viewer of the painting), the bird seemed to tilt as if stepping into the room.

This was the painting "Nevermore," by Paul Gauguin. Poe had inspired other artists and poets as well, such as Manet and Baudelaire. The exhibits in the small room at the top of the stairs touched on Poe's influence around the world. The girls sat down on benches arranged to view the exhibited artwork. It was in this room that their father had read them "The Tell-Tale Heart."

Grace was strangely silent.

"What's the matter?" asked Kate, looking intently at her sister. Without realizing it, Grace had a deep frown on her face. She looked at her sister and started to get tears in her eyes.

"I don't know why we're doing all of this. It was fun at first, but not now. Not with Poe. Poe is not a fun guy. He dwells too much on loss and loneliness and death."

Kate hesitated. "He did seem to be hard to get along with," she agreed. "He even accused Longfellow of plagiarism."

Grace seemed to be getting more upset. Kate waited.

"Why did Dad bring us here?" Suddenly, Grace burst into tears.

Kate reached out to her sister. Typically, Kate was not a touchy-feely person, but her sister was obviously grieving. The themes of loss and death in Poe's work, and indeed his life, had brought their own losses to the surface. "It's okay," she said as she put a hand on her sister's back. "Things aren't the way they used to be. In many ways, they never will be. That's true. We've just got to deal with things as best we can and go on with living. I know that's what Dad would have wanted. I think that's why he did all this."

Grace sobbed, but nodded. Kate watched as her sister visibly took control of her emotions.

"Catharsis?" Grace asked. She had studied classical views of theater as catharsis, but she had never really understood it until now. Grace's fingers began to tingle as she hyperventilated. She felt odd.

She could feel her mind expanding. She began to see connections everywhere: Poe and Longfellow facing each other on the mantelpiece at Maymont. The childless Dooleys' legacy of beauty and charity versus the childless Macbeths' legacy of hatred and violence. Iambic pentameter: "The boy who went to war returned a man." We will not live forever.

Grace blinked several times as she wiped away her tears.

Kate said, "Let's go home."

Chapter Seventeen

Home

Home. As she drove, Grace reflected on the term. As she had moved into a wider world, she had begun to see her home as an extension of herself, not simply a building that she occupied.

She thought of Richmond. Richmond, like Rome—she grinned a little—was a city built on hills. It was on what was now Libby Hill that William Byrd had looked east down the James River and been reminded of the view from Richmond Hill, in the English town of Richmond-on-the-Thames. From the Chesapeake Bay, ships could travel dozens of nautical miles inland up the James River, until it became shallow and rocky at the falls of Richmond-on-the-James. From Powhatan Hill, which became Richmond Hill, which became Church Hill, one could see the inexorable transition of the land as those who made it their home changed from native peoples to adventurers to modern communities.

Richmond was the capital of the state that gave rise to a nation, but Richmond was not a perfect city. Arising on land occupied by the Powhatan tribe, funded by tobacco, capital of the Confederacy that had fought to maintain an economy based on the work of enslaved persons, Richmond had mirrored much of the passionate conflict of the nation. However, Richmond had also produced the nation's first African-American governor, the first African-American female bank president, and the first African-American Wimbledon champion. Descendants of the Powhatan tribes still lived in and around Richmond. Richmond was the beloved home of the nation's first chief justice. George Washington built Richmond's canals. Thomas Jefferson designed Richmond's capitol building. Richmond was the resting place of presidents, generals, authors, actors, scholars, and other people of renown and distinction. Richmond was a crossroads: the Northside versus the Southside; the West End versus the East End; historically black areas versus historically white areas.

In many cultures, crossroads were almost magical places of decision and consequence. Grace felt she was at a crossroads in her own life. Not only did she need to decide which direction her studies were to take, she felt as if she was on the threshold of being a different person. She had grown, not only physically, but in some deeper, perhaps even spiritual way. She found the change hard to articulate even to herself, but it had happened. She wasn't the little girl who was afraid of Howl-O-Scream any longer.

Grace turned her car onto Laurel Street. Her dad's father had grown up on Laurel Street, in Oregon Hill. Another of the hills of Richmond, Oregon Hill was the home of generations of blue-collar families. The roots of those who lived there ran very deep. Everyone who lived there seemed to have a nickname, like Poogie, Pee Wee, Stinky, or Gimpy. Grace had lost count of the times she had heard family stories about the place. Richmond had been the first city in the United States to have electric streetcars, and Grace's grandfather had delighted in telling the story of how he and his gang would soap the tracks so that the streetcars couldn't get up Oregon Hill. It was on that hill that Grace's grandfather had raised pigeons on the roof of his row house. He had a ferocious rabbit named Bunny-Boo that, it was said, could beat any dog in the neighborhood. The beast would corner neighbors in their own yards, until Grace's grandfather came to retrieve the gigantic lagomorph.

And then there was Hollywood Cemetery.

At once spectacular and peaceful, Hollywood Cemetery was not a place of grieving or gloom. Instead, it was a beautiful place of rest and remembrance.

Turning right off of Laurel Street, Grace saw the entrance. She had many fond memories of walking through Hollywood Cemetery with her father and sister. Today, however, she was alone.

It did not surprise her at all that her father had wished to rest at Hollywood Cemetery. The grounds felt more like an outdoor museum or park, and the statuary and landscaping reminded Grace of the grounds at Maymont. The view of the James River was lovely. Despite missing her father, Grace couldn't really be gloomy in this place. She supposed it was a bit odd to call a cemetery "cool," but this place was cool. She was glad her father rested here.

Before his death, her dad had also mentioned that he wanted to rest near one of his heroes, Douglas Southall Freeman, who had written Pulitzer Prize-winning books in his spare time, despite having a full-time job as editor of the Richmond News Leader daily paper. Grace hoped that her dad would not have been disappointed that they hadn't erected a monumental likeness of himself with his finger in the air, as he had (jokingly?) requested. But he did have a nice marker.

She left some flowers by his marker and paused a moment to reflect on what was present beneath it. She did not really feel that he was there. His body might be there, but somehow, she felt that he was not.

Grace turned away from the grave and made her

way over to the pyramid. Located in the Confederate area, the stone pyramid was an impressive sight. The stones, many still bearing excavation marks, had been arranged in a dry stack, with no mortar to bind them. Legend had it that a convicted horse thief had been given his freedom for bravely placing the capstone.

Grace wandered around the pyramid, looking at the markers. She remembered how she and Kate had looked at these same markers as children, trying to get new ideas for characters in their stories from the unique names on the stones. Now, years later, it finally struck Grace that a place such as Hollywood Cemetery could be an inspiration for art. Perhaps Death was the mother of Beauty after all.

Chapter Eighteen

The Final Clue

Several days passed. The summer days were growing shorter, and Grace could smell fall in the air. Very soon, she would have to go back to school. Kate had already returned to her work. The adventures that they had shared this summer were coming to an end. She felt it. Soon the treasure hunt would be done.

Then an envelope came in the mail. Grace held it, feeling the contents through the envelope. A sturdy card was inside. Part of her didn't want the hunt to be finished, but most of her knew it was time.

Grace opened the envelope. It was a Fourth of July card. Inside was written:

They met in Richmond
One rests with Bunker Hill soil
Edgar Allan Poe

"Haiku. Appropriate," Grace said aloud. Poe had considered himself first and foremost a poet. She wanted to call Kate, but knew that her sister was busy with her dissertation.

Grace looked at the clue. Two people; one was Poe. "The other rests"—meaning, is buried? —"in Bunker Hill." The card was an Independence Day card. That would fit. But Grace frowned. No, she thought, the other rests not in Bunker Hill soil, but with Bunker Hill soil. This implied that the person rested elsewhere.

Grace went to her computer and searched for information on the Battle of Bunker Hill. She found that on June 17, 1775, Colonial troops commanded by William Prescott had occupied and fortified Bunker Hill and Breed's Hill during the siege of Boston, Massachusetts. When the British realized that the hills had been fortified, they attacked. Most of the battle had taken place on Breed's Hill, though Bunker Hill may have been a British objective. Although the British had ultimately won the battle, the victory came at a great cost. The British forces sustained 800 wounded and 226 dead, many of whom had been officers. With the cost of victory greater than what was gained, the outcome was considered a Pyrrhic victory. Though for them it was technically a loss, the Colonial forces had proved, perhaps most importantly to themselves, that they could survive a pitched battle with British troops. "Don't fire until you see the whites of their eyes" had become a memorable quote from the battle, although it was unclear who had actually said it.

Grace read about the impact and effects of the Battle of Bunker Hill. She was about to move on when something caught her eye. On June 17, 1825, at the fiftieth anniversary celebration of the Battle of Bunker Hill, the Marquis de Lafayette had laid the cornerstone of the Bunker Hill Monument. Daniel Webster had spoken at the ceremony. A footnote mentioned that when the Marquis de Lafayette had died, he was buried next to his wife at the Cimetiere de Picpus, under soil from Bunker Hill, which his son Georges sprinkled upon him.

Grace blinked. "They met in Richmond," she said. She typed a few more queries into her computer. "'In 1824, Poe was part of the honor guard that welcomed the Marquis de Lafayette to Richmond.'" She took a few deep breaths. "'He rests...'"

Grace cooked, taking her time. In Kate's honor, she made everything vegetarian: roasted beets and radishes, kale, twice-baked potatoes, steamed asparagus with cheese, and pull-apart bread. Mom insisted on providing dessert: fruit tarts, which had long been one of her favorites. They talked and enjoyed each other's company.

"How goes the treasure hunt?" Mom asked.

Grace looked at Kate, then said, "We've solved the last puzzle."

That was news to Kate. "We have?" she exclaimed. "What is it?"

Grace explained about the card. The chain of evidence was this:

The Old Stone House, which held the...

Poe Museum, which commemorated...

Edgar Allan Poe, who, in 1824 met...

The Marquis de Lafayette, who was buried with soil from Bunker Hill in...

Paris, which in 1987 was the brief home of language student...

Mom.

Grace smiled a gentle smile and said to her mother, "Tell us about Paris."

Chapter Nineteen

The Good Friend

Within a few days, a different type of note came. Along with it, inside the envelope, came a gift card to Can Can. The note said to call the provided number for further instructions. The girls called.

Dressed in a suit, he sat at a table alone. His hair was gray. The girls recognized him from their dad's funeral.

Frank Harrington had been one of the pallbearers, along with Dad's brothers and nephews. Mom said that he had been Dad's best friend for almost their entire lives: they had met when Dad was in high school, and remained close throughout their adult years. Kate and Grace both remembered Dad's frequent trips to breakfast with his friend. Although the girls vaguely remembered coming on some of the trips, the meetings were usually reserved just for the two friends. Dad and Frank's relationship had been so profound that they'd almost had their own language, and could evoke a smile in each other with just a phrase or a barely intelligible sound.

Now, as adults themselves, the girls were glad that their dad had experienced a deep and lifelong friendship with the man seated before them. Although he seemed a bit stiff and uncomfortable with the circumstances, he came across as kind and pleasant as he looked at the pair of them and began to speak.

"Hello, Kate. Hello, Grace. I see that you received your dad's letters, including the last one. I bet you wondered how he did this. He gave me instructions to mail his letters out at specific intervals, which I did. Your dad asked me to carry out these rather extraordinary instructions one year after his death. He asked that I keep this plan of his confidential until the end, if at all possible. In the event that I could not carry out his instructions, we made other arrangements for you to receive these." He tapped two packages wrapped in, of all things, Easter-bunny paper. Identical letters sat atop the packages, each letter clearly marked for the recipient.

"But as it turned out, things went as he planned." Frank stood up. "I miss your dad a lot. I'm sure you do, too. If there is ever anything you need, please contact me." He gave them his card. "For now, I am going to follow your father's last request and leave you with these."

He handed each of the girls one of the wrapped packages, then nodded farewell. The girls looked at each other, and opened their letters.

Chapter Twenty

Kate and Grace

The letters read:

My Sweet Girls,
I hope you had a good time on your Adventures. Please thank my good friend Frank for his help in this undertaking. I hope everything unfolded as I planned. As someone probably said, this is just the sort of thing that I would do. I had fun creating these puzzles for you. The thought of all of these shenanigans kept me going through some tough moments.

Before you are the journals I have kept for you for your entire lives. I bet you wondered what happened to them. Well, here they are. In them I documented, from my standpoint of course, many of the important events, both mundane and momentous, that occurred over the course of your young lives. In the front of each book, you will also find gold coins that your mother gave to me throughout our marriage. REAL TREASURE. I will leave it to you to decide which of these things is more valuable.

The treasure is nice, of course, but my overall purpose in bringing you two together was to reintroduce you to each other and, hopefully, instill in you the habit of coming together regularly to share in each other's lives. I also wanted to impress upon you both how important your mother is. Take care of her. Spend time with her. Honor my original sweet girl and help her as she ages.

And now for some Dad advice:

Keep your debt low. Nothing makes you as vulnerable in this world as debt.

Be careful in your relationships. If a

relationship brings you comfort and joy, embrace it. If a relationship brings you anxiety, reevaluate it.

Friendship and loyalty are very important in life, but should not be blind.

As my dad taught me, make time for yourself and time for your family in this busy world.

Character matters.

Be good to people. But remember, being good and being nice are not the same thing.

Try to do what you feel is right. Others may disagree, but sticking to what you believe in is one example of courage.

Smoking is bad for your health.

Drugs, like alcohol, can affect your judgment and memory. They can alter your behavior and allow decisions or actions that you may later regret or that could harm you.

Be compassionate.

Exercise regularly and stay active.

Do things.

Work hard. But remember, work is not who you are. No one ever dies saying, "I wish I had spent more time at work."

Remember, when all is said and done, all you really leave as proof that you were ever here is your family and your art.

Although the world can be painful at times, your life can and should be full of joy and wonder and fun.

Now, although I am reluctant to do so, I must say my final Goodbye. Before I go, let me say this: if you are ever feeling small and insignificant, remember that in all the history of all the people of the world, only I could have done this.

Take care, my sweet girls.

Love,
Dad

P.S. If you keep your eyes open for your new favorite thing, any day can be a Friday Adventure.

Chapter Twenty-One

Friday Adventures

Months had passed since they had met Dad's friend at Can Can, and now, Kate and Grace found themselves returning. They had settled into a routine of getting together frequently for meals and talk. They spoke of boyfriends and work, plans and disappointments. Sometimes their mom would join them.

Kate had finished her master's program and was now pursuing her PhD in biology. Grace was working toward graduation from college and was active in the theater. She wanted to direct and ultimately make movies.

Today, as they slid into their usual seats at the bar, both girls ordered appetizers.

"I'll have the cheese plate," Kate said.

"And I'll start with onion soup." After placing her order, Grace turned to her sister and took a deep breath. "I got the part," she beamed. As usual, she had delayed speaking the news until the last possible second, for effect.

"I knew you would get it," Kate said as she smiled benevolently at her sister. "Good for you. When do rehearsals start?"

"Right away. I hope I can manage all those lines."

"With your memory, that should be a piece of cake."

"Speaking of cake, are we having dessert today to celebrate your big news?" Grace grinned.

Kate felt a blush rise to her cheeks. A deep feeling of satisfaction warmed her. She had worked for months on the paper describing a new species of canopy beetle in Costa Rica, and it had finally been published in a respected science journal, with her name listed as one of the authors. That publication would pave the road to her PhD application, which was being submitted as they spoke. But even more than that, to hear her sister speak with sincere appreciation for her work made her feel good.

"Yes, I think today is a dessert day," Kate said with a crooked grin.

Their appetizers came, along with the wonderful warm French bread that they both ate with relish. With the clinks of glasses and the tings of forks on plates in the background, the girls—the sweet girls—looked at each other and smiled.

About the Author

PV Jackson is a native of Richmond, Virginia. He received his undergraduate degree in religion from the College of William and Mary and a bachelor of science, master of education, and doctorate of medicine from Virginia Commonwealth University. For more than twenty years he has worked as a primary care physician and medical educator in the Richmond area. He lives with his wife and daughters in Midlothian, Virginia.

Acknowledgments

This is a work of fiction, although real landmarks of the culturally rich town of Richmond, Virginia, are lovingly portrayed therein.

I wish to acknowledge those who helped in the execution of this book:

Helen Warriner-Burke, docent at Maymont, who led my tour of Maymont House and provided valuable information and introductions.

Thomas Burke, who kindly shared his memories of growing up on Oregon Hill in Richmond.

Ehren Ziegler, for his excellent podcast, "Chop Bard." His enthusiasm, experience, and insights into Shakespeare opened my eyes to this fascinating world.

Stuart Jackson, who has long been the repository of family lore and stories. Many joyful memories of laughter reside within generations of our family at the retelling (for the umpteenth time) of family stories. Ruth Atkinson, for her encouragement, critical eye, and shared love of books.

Michele and Meghann Sayles, who provided honest and much-appreciated suggestions and insight.

Barbara Carper and Doug Klassett, for sharing their experiences of Costa Rica.

KR Jackson for the cover art.

Annie Tobey, for her proofreading and guidance.

Robert Pruett of Brandylane Publishers, Inc.

Profound thanks to my wife for her patient editing.

A special thanks to my dad, who inspired this book by taking me, as a boy, on our own version of Friday Adventures.

References

Swannanoa:http://en.wikipedia.org/wiki/Swannanoa_(mansion)

James H. Dooley: http://en.wikipedia.org/wiki/James_H._Dooley

Maymont: http://en.wikipedia.org/wiki/Maymont

O'Leary, E. L. (2003). From Morning to Night. Domestic Service in Maymont House and the Gilded Age South. Charlottesville and London. University of Virginia Press.

Loch Ness: http://en.wikipedia.org/wiki/Loch_Ness

Loch Ness Monster: http://en.wikipedia.org/wiki/Loch_Ness_Monster

Descartes, R. (2006). A Discourse on the Method. (Ian Maclean, Trans). Oxford. Oxford University Press. (Original work published 1637)

Inverness: http://en.wikipedia.org/wiki/Inverness

Macbeth, King of Scotland: http://en.wikipedia.org/wiki/Macbeth,_King_of_Scotland

Macbeth: http://www.inyourearshakespeare.com/www. inyourearshakespeare.com//plays/macbeth/macMain.html

Shakespeare, W. (2000), Macbeth. (Orgel, S. & Braunmuller, A.R., Editors). New York. Penguin Putnam. (Original work published in 1623)

Ziegler, E. (2011). Devouring Shakespeare. Copyright 2008 Shannon Sneedse.

Agecroft Hall: http://en.wikipedia.org/wiki/Agecroft_Hall

John of Gaunt: http://en.wikipedia.org/wiki/John_of_Gaunt

"This blessed plot..."Act II, scene i, 42–54, The Tragedy of King Richard II (at Wikisource)

Globe Theatre: http://en.wikipedia.org/wiki/Globe_Theatre

Rose Theatre: http://en.wikipedia.org/wiki/The_Rose_(theatre)

Edward the Confessor: http://en.wikipedia.org/wiki/Edward_the_Confessor

Crutchfield, L. (2012). Agecroft Hall. Richmond, Virginia. Agecroft Association

Mitchell, R. M. (2013). Richmond's The Old Stone House. Its History and How It Became the Edgar Allan Poe Museum. Copyright c. 2013 by Rose Marie Mitchell. oshbook@gmail.com

Poe: http://en.wikipedia.org/wiki/Edgar_Allan_Poe
  http://poestories.com/timeline.php
  http://www.eapoe.org/pstudies/ps1970/p1973101.htm

Fisher, B.F. (2008). The Cambridge Introduction to Edgar Allan Poe. Cambridge. Cambridge University Press.

Dupin: http://en.wikipedia.org/wiki/C._Auguste_Dupin

Richmond: http://en.wikipedia.org/wiki/Richmond,_Virginia

Lafayette: http://en.wikipedia.org/wiki/Gilbert_du_Motier,_Marquis_de_Lafayette

Douglas Southall Freeman: http://en.wikipedia.org/wiki/Douglas_Southall_Freeman

Hollywood Cemetery: http://www.hollywoodcemetery.org/
http://en.wikipedia.org/wiki/Hollywood_Cemetery_(Richmond,_Virginia)

Peters, J.O. (2010). Richmond's Hollywood Cemetery. Petersburg. Dietz Press

Poe and Manet: http://rmc.library.cornell.edu/poe/

Cuvier: http://en.wikipedia.org/wiki/Georges_Cuvier

Gauguin Nevermore: http://upload.wikimedia.org/wikipedia/commons/9/9f/Paul_Gauguin_091.jpg

Richmond Theatre Fire 1811: http://en.wikipedia.org/wiki/Richmond_Theatre_fire

Bunker Hill: http://en.wikipedia.org/wiki/Battle_of_Bunker_Hill

www.ingramcontent.com/pod-product-compliance
Lightning Source LLC
Chambersburg PA
CBHW050802250626
47155CB00005B/2176